# Dear Parent:
## Your child's love of reading starts here!

Every child learns to read in a different way and at his or her own speed. Some go back and forth between reading levels and read favorite books again and again. Others read through each level in order. You can help your young reader improve and become more confident by encouraging his or her own interests and abilities. From books your child reads with you to the first books he or she reads alone, there are I Can Read Books for every stage of reading:

**SHARED READING**
Basic language, word repetition, and whimsical illustrations, ideal for sharing with your emergent reader

**BEGINNING READING**
Short sentences, familiar words, and simple concepts for children eager to read on their own

**READING WITH HELP**
Engaging stories, longer sentences, and language play for developing readers

**READING ALONE**
Complex plots, challenging vocabulary, and high-interest topics for the independent reader

**ADVANCED READING**
Short paragraphs, chapters, and exciting themes for the perfect bridge to chapter books

**I Can Read Books** have introduced children to the joy of reading since 1957. Featuring award-winning authors and illustrators and a fabulous cast of beloved characters, I Can Read Books set the standard for beginning readers.

A lifetime of discovery begins with the magical words **"I Can Read!"**

*Visit www.icanread.com for information*
*on enriching your child's reading experience.*

I Can Read!™ SHARED My First READING

# JUST HELPING
# MY DAD

BEST
WATER
SAVER
TOILET

# BY MERCER MAYER

**HARPER**
*An Imprint of HarperCollinsPublishers*

To Arden and his little boy, Braelynn

I Can Read Book® is a trademark of HarperCollins Publishers.

Library of Congress catalog card number: 2010936234
ISBN 978-0-06-083564-4 (trade bdg.) — ISBN 978-0-06-083563-7 (pbk.)

Typography by Diane Dubreuil
11   12   13     LP/WOR      10   9   8   7   6   5   4   3   2
❖
First Edition

A Big Tuna Trading Company, LLC/J.R. Sansevere Book
www.littlecritter.com

Dad is home today.

I will help my dad do things.

"Wake up, Dad," I say.

"We have work to do."

Dad is sleepy.

I make breakfast for him

all by myself.

I am helping Dad.

I cut the grass.

Oops! The mower got away!
"Sorry, Dad," I say.

I wash the car, just for Dad.

# Who left the windows open?

I can paint.

14

But Dad has to finish.

15

I see a bees' nest.

"I will fix it, Dad," I call.

Dad is yelling something.
"Run!" Dad yells. "Run!"
I run fast.

We go to town,
just Dad and me.

We buy gas.

I say, "Dad, I can pump gas."

Dad pumps the gas.

We go to the store.

I get stuff for Dad.

"Too much, Dad?" I ask.

Dad needs a new hammer.
"This hammer really works!
Sorry about the nails," I say.

We get a parking ticket.
Dad does not look happy.

Dad says, "I am not mad,
just not happy."
I say, "That's fair, Dad."

We go home.

Mom says, "The toilet is broken."

"I will fix it," I say.

# I can't fix it. I call Dad.

I forgot to turn off the hose.
I say, "That's okay, Dad.
Grass loves water!"

We have dinner. Then
Dad and I watch a movie.

# Dad is tired.

It's time to sleep.
Dad tucks me in.

"Did I help you, Dad?" I ask.
Dad says, "Yes, you did.
Thank you."

What a great day,
just helping my dad!